THE BAT-POET

to Mary

THE BAT-POET

By RANDALL JARRELL

Pictures by Maurice Sendak

 COLLIER BOOKS
Division of Macmillan Publishing Co., Inc.
New York

Macmillan Publishing Co., Inc.
866 Third Avenue, New York, N.Y. 10022
Collier Macmillan Canada, Ltd.

The Bat-Poet is published in a hardcover edition by Macmillan Publishing Co., Inc.

Printed in the United States of America
First Collier Books Edition 1977
10 9 8 7 6 5 4 3 2

LIBRARY OF CONGRESS CATALOGING IN PUBLICATION DATA

Jarrell, Randall, 1914–1965.
    The bat-poet.

    SUMMARY: A bat who can't sleep days makes up poems about the woodland creatures he now perceives for the first time.
    [1. Bats—Fiction.   2. Animals—Fiction]
I. Sendak, Maurice. II. Title.
PZ7.J295Bat6   [Fic]   76–17823
ISBN 0–02–043910–5

Once upon a time there was a bat—a little light brown bat, the color of coffee with cream in it. He looked like a furry mouse with wings. When I'd go in and out my front door, in the daytime, I'd look up over my head and see him hanging upside down from the roof of the porch. He and the others hung there in a bunch, all snuggled together with their wings folded, fast asleep. Sometimes one of them would wake up for a minute and get in a more comfortable position, and then the others would wriggle around in their sleep till they'd got more comfortable too; when they all moved it looked as if a fur wave went over them. At night they'd fly up and down, around and around, and catch insects and eat them; on a rainy night, though, they'd stay snuggled together just as though it were still day. If you pointed a flashlight at them you'd see them screw up their faces to keep the light out of their eyes.

Toward the end of summer all the bats except the little brown one began sleeping in the barn. He missed them, and tried to get them to come back and sleep on the porch with him. "What do you want to sleep in the barn for?" he asked them.

"We don't know," the others said. "What do you want to sleep on the porch for?"

"It's where we always sleep," he said. "If I slept in the barn I'd be homesick. Do come back and sleep with me!" But they wouldn't.

So he had to sleep all alone. He missed the others. They had always felt so warm and furry against him; whenever he'd waked, he'd pushed himself up into the middle of them and gone right back to sleep. Now he'd wake up and, instead of snuggling against the others and going back to sleep, he would just hang there and think. Sometimes he would open his eyes a little and look out into the sunlight. It gave him a queer feeling for it to be daytime and for him to be hanging there looking; he felt the way you would feel if you woke up and went to the window and stayed there for hours, looking out into the moonlight.

It was different in the daytime. The squirrels and

2

the chipmunk, that he had never seen before—at night they were curled up in their nests or holes, fast asleep—ate nuts and acorns and seeds, and ran after each other, playing. And all the birds hopped and

sang and flew; at night they had been asleep, except for the mockingbird. The bat had always heard the mockingbird. The mockingbird would sit on the highest branch of a tree, in the moonlight, and sing half the night. The bat loved to listen to him. He could imitate all the other birds—he'd even imitate the way the squirrels chattered when they were angry, like two rocks being knocked together; and he could imitate the milk bottles being put down on the porch and the barn door closing, a long rusty squeak. And he made up songs and words all his own, that nobody else had ever said or sung.

The bat told the other bats about all the things you could see and hear in the daytime. "You'd love them," he said. "The next time you wake up in the daytime, just keep your eyes open for a while and don't go back to sleep."

The other bats were sure they wouldn't like that. "We wish we didn't wake up at all," they said. "When you wake up in the daytime the light hurts your eyes—the thing to do is to close them and go right back to sleep. Day's to sleep in; as soon as it's night we'll open our eyes."

"But won't you even try it?" the little brown bat said. "Just for once, try it."

The bats all said: "No."

"But why not?" asked the little brown bat.

The bats said: "We don't know. We just don't want to."

"At least listen to the mockingbird. When you hear him it's just like the daytime."

The other bats said: "He sounds so queer. If only he squeaked or twittered—but he keeps shouting in that bass voice of his." They said this because the mockingbird's voice sounded terribly loud and deep to them; they always made little high twittering sounds themselves.

"Once you get used to it you'll like it," the little bat said. "Once you get used to it, it sounds wonderful."

"All right," said the others, "we'll try." But they were just being polite; they didn't try.

The little brown bat kept waking up in the daytime, and kept listening to the mockingbird, until

4

one day he thought: "*I could make up a song like the mockingbird's.*" But when he tried, his high notes were all high and his low notes were all high and the notes in between were all high: he couldn't make a tune. So he imitated the mockingbird's words instead. At first his words didn't go together—even the bat could see that they didn't sound a bit like the mockingbird's. But after a while some of them began to sound beautiful, so that the bat said to himself: "If you get the words right you don't need a tune."

The bat went over and over his words till he could say them off by heart. That night he said them to the other bats. "I've made the words like the mockingbird's," he told them, "so you can tell what it's like in the daytime." Then he said to them in a deep voice—he couldn't help imitating the mockingbird—his words about the daytime:

> At dawn, the sun shines like a million moons
> And all the shadows are as bright as moonlight.
> The birds begin to sing with all their might.
> The world awakens and forgets the night.
>
> The black-and-gray turns green-and-gold-and-blue.
> The squirrels begin to—

But when he'd got this far the other bats just couldn't keep quiet any longer.

"The sun *hurts*," said one. "It hurts like getting something in your eyes."

"That's right," said another. "And shadows are black—how can a shadow be bright?"

Another one said: "What's green-and-gold-and-blue? When you say things like that we don't know what you mean."

"And it's just not real," the first one said. "When the sun rises the world goes to sleep."

"But go on," said one of the others. "We didn't mean to interrupt you."

"No, we're sorry we interrupted you," all the others said. "Say us the rest."

But when the bat tried to say them the rest he couldn't remember a word. It was hard to say anything at all, but finally he said: "I—I—tomorrow I'll

say you the rest." Then he flew back to the porch. There were lots of insects flying around the light, but he didn't catch a one; instead he flew to his rafter, hung there upside down with his wings folded, and after a while went to sleep.

But he kept on making poems like the mocking-bird's—only now he didn't say them to the bats. One night he saw a mother possum, with all her little white baby possums holding tight to her, eating the fallen apples under the apple tree; one night an owl swooped down on him and came so close he'd have caught him if the bat hadn't flown into a hole in the old oak by the side of the house; and another time four squirrels spent the whole morning chasing each other up and down trees, across the lawn, and over the roof. He made up poems about them all. Sometimes the poem would make him think: "It's like the mockingbird. This time it's really like the mockingbird!" But sometimes the poem would seem so bad to him that he'd get discouraged and stop in the middle, and by the next day he'd have forgotten it.

When he would wake up in the daytime and hang there looking out at the colors of the world, he would say the poems over to himself. He wanted to say them to the other bats, but then he would remember what had happened when he'd said them before. There was nobody for him to say the poems to.

One day he thought: "I could say them to the mockingbird." It got to be a regular thought of his. It was a long time, though, before he really went to the mockingbird.

The mockingbird had bad days when he would try to drive everything out of the yard, no matter what it was. He always had a peremptory, authoritative look, as if he were more alive than anything else and wanted everything else to know it; on his bad days he'd dive on everything that came into the yard—on cats and dogs, even—and strike at them with his little sharp beak and sharp claws. On his good days he didn't pay so much attention to the world, but just sang.

The day the bat went to him the mockingbird was perched on the highest branch of the big willow by the porch, singing with all his might. He was a clear gray, with white bars across his wings that flashed when he flew; every part of him had a clear, quick, decided look about it. He was standing on tiptoe, singing and singing and singing; sometimes he'd spring up into the air. This time he was singing a song about mockingbirds.

The bat fluttered to the nearest branch, hung upside down from it, and listened; finally when the mockingbird stopped for a moment he said in his little high voice: "It's beautiful, just beautiful!"

"You like poetry?" asked the mockingbird. You could tell from the way he said it that he was surprised.

"I love it," said the bat. "I listen to you every night. Every day too. I—I—"

"It's the last poem I've composed," said the mockingbird. "It's called 'To a Mockingbird.'"

"It's wonderful," the bat said. "Wonderful! Of all the songs I ever heard you sing, it's the best."

This pleased the mockingbird—mockingbirds love

to be told that their last song is the best. "I'll sing it for you again," the mockingbird offered.

"Oh, please do sing it again," said the bat. "I'd love to hear it again. Just love to! Only when you've finished could I—"

But the mockingbird had already started. He not only sang it again, he made up new parts, and sang them over and over and over; they were so beautiful that the bat forgot about his own poem and just listened. When the mockingbird had finished, the bat thought: "No, I just can't say him mine. Still, though—" He said to the mockingbird: "It's wonderful to get to hear you. I could listen to you forever."

"It's a pleasure to sing to such a responsive audience," said the mockingbird. "Any time you'd like to hear it again just tell me."

The bat said: "Could—could—"

"Yes?" said the mockingbird.

The bat went on in a shy voice: "Do you suppose that I—that I could—"

The mockingbird said warmly: "That you could hear it again? Of course you can. I'll be delighted." And he sang it all over again. This time it was the best of all.

The bat told him so, and the mockingbird looked pleased but modest; it was easy for him to look pleased but hard for him to look modest, he was so full of himself. The bat asked him: "Do you suppose a bat could make poems like yours?"

"A *bat?*" the mockingbird said. But then he went on politely, "Well, I don't see why not. He couldn't sing them, of course—he simply doesn't have the range; but that's no reason he couldn't make them up. Why, I suppose for bats a bat's poems would be ideal."

The bat said: "Sometimes when I wake up in the daytime I make up poems. Could I—I wonder whether I could say you one of *my* poems?"

A queer look came over the mockingbird's face, but he said cordially: "I'd be delighted to hear one. Go right ahead." He settled himself on his branch with a listening expression.

The bat said:

A shadow is floating through the moonlight.
Its wings don't make a sound.
Its claws are long, its beak is bright.
Its eyes try all the corners of the night.

It calls and calls: all the air swells and heaves
And washes up and down like water.
The ear that listens to the owl believes
In death. The bat beneath the eaves,

The mouse beside the stone are still as death—
The owl's air washes them like water.
The owl goes back and forth inside the night,
And the night holds its breath.

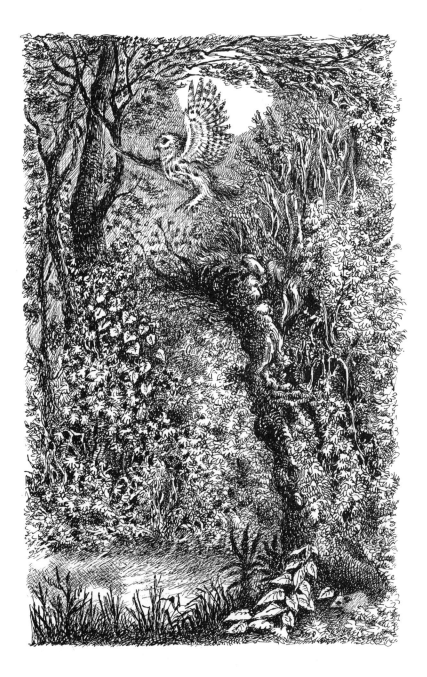

When he'd finished his poem the bat waited for the mockingbird to say something; he didn't know it, but he was holding his breath.

"Why, I like it," said the mockingbird. "Technically it's quite accomplished. The way you change the rhyme-scheme's particularly effective."

The bat said: "It is?"

"Oh yes," said the mockingbird. "And it was clever of you to have that last line two feet short."

The bat said blankly: "Two feet short?"

"It's two feet short," said the mockingbird a little impatiently. "The next-to-the-last line's iambic pentameter, and the last line's iambic trimeter."

The bat looked so bewildered that the mockingbird said in a kind voice: "An iambic foot has one weak syllable and one strong syllable; the weak one comes first. That last line of yours has six syllables and the one before it has ten: when you shorten the last line like that it gets the effect of the night holding its breath."

"I didn't know that," the bat said. "I just made it like holding your breath."

"To be sure, to be sure!" said the mockingbird. "I enjoyed your poem very much. When you've made up some more do come round and say me another."

The bat said that he would, and fluttered home to his rafter. Partly he felt very good—the mockingbird had liked his poem—and partly he felt just terrible. He thought: "Why, I might as well have said it to

14

the bats. What do I care how many feet it has? The owl nearly kills me, and he says he likes the rhyme-scheme!" He hung there upside down, thinking bitterly. After a while he said to himself: "The trouble isn't making poems, the trouble's finding somebody that will listen to them."

Before he went to sleep he said his owl-poem over to himself, and it seemed to him that it was exactly like the owl. "The *owl* would like it," he thought. "If only I could say it to the owl!"

And then he thought: "That's it! I can't say it to the owl, I don't dare get that near him; but if I made up a poem about the chipmunk I could say it to the chipmunk—*he'd* be interested." The bat got so excited his fur stood up straight and he felt warm all over. He thought: "I'll go to the chipmunk and say, 'If you'll give me six crickets I'll make a poem about you.' Really I'd do it for nothing; but they don't respect something if they get it for nothing. I'll say: 'For six crickets I'll do your portrait in verse.'"

The next day, at twilight, the bat flew to the chipmunk's hole. The chipmunk had dozens of holes, but the bat had noticed that there was one he liked best and always slept in. Before long the chipmunk ran up, his cheeks bulging. "Hello," said the bat.

The instant he heard the bat the chipmunk froze; then he dived into his hole. "Wait! Wait!" the bat cried. But the chipmunk had disappeared. "Come back," the bat called. "I won't hurt you." But he had

to talk for a long time before the chipmunk came back, and even then he just stuck the tip of his nose out of the hole.

The bat hardly knew how to begin, but he timidly said to the chipmunk, who listened timidly: "I thought of making this offer to—to the animals of the vicinity. You're the first one I've made it to."

The chipmunk didn't say anything. The bat

16

gulped, and said quickly: "For only six crickets I'll do your portrait in verse."

The chipmunk said: "What are crickets?"

The bat felt discouraged. "I knew I might have to tell him about poems," he thought, "but I never thought I'd have to tell him about *crickets*." He explained: "They're little black things you see on the porch at night, by the light. They're awfully good. But that's all right about them; instead of crickets you could give me—well, this time you don't have to give me anything. It's a—an introductory offer."

The chipmunk said in a friendly voice: "I don't understand."

"I'll make you a poem about yourself," said the bat. "One just about you." He saw from the look in the chipmunk's eyes that the chipmunk didn't understand. The bat said: "I'll say you a poem about the owl, and then you'll see what it's like."

He said his poem and the chipmunk listened intently; when the poem was over the chipmunk gave a big shiver and said, "It's terrible, just terrible! Is there really something like that at night?"

The bat said: "If it weren't for that hole in the oak he'd have got *me*."

The chipmunk said in a determined voice: "I'm going to bed earlier. Sometimes when there're lots of nuts I stay out till it's pretty dark; but believe me, I'm never going to again."

The bat said: "It's a pleasure to say a poem to—to

such a responsive audience. Do you want me to start on the poem about you?"

The chipmunk said thoughtfully: "I don't have enough holes. It'd be awfully easy to dig some more holes."

"Shall I start on the poem about you?" asked the bat.

"All right," said the chipmunk. "But could you put in lots of holes? The first thing in the morning I'm going to dig myself another."

"I'll put in a lot," the bat promised. "Is there anything else you'd like to have in it?"

The chipmunk thought for a minute and said,

"Well, nuts. And seeds—those big fat seeds they have in the feeder."

"All right," said the bat. "Tomorrow afternoon I'll be back. Or day after tomorrow—I don't really know how long it will take." He and the chipmunk said good-by to each other and he fluttered home to the porch. As soon as he got comfortably settled he started to work on the poem about the chipmunk. But somehow he kept coming back to the poem about the owl, and what the chipmunk had said, and how he'd looked. "*He* didn't say any of that two-feet-short stuff," the bat thought triumphantly; "*he* was scared!" The bat hung there upside down, trying to work on his new poem. He was happy.

When at last he'd finished the poem—it took him longer than he'd thought—he went looking for the chipmunk. It was a bright afternoon, and the sun blazed in the bat's eyes, so that everything looked blurred and golden. When he met the chipmunk hurrying down the path that ran past the old stump, he thought: "What a beautiful color he is! Why, the fur back by his tail's rosy, almost. And those lovely black and white stripes on his back!"

"Hello," he said.

"Hello," said the chipmunk. "Is it done yet?"

"All done," said the bat happily. "I'll say it to you. It's named 'The Chipmunk's Day.'"

The chipmunk said in a pleased voice: "My day." He sat there and listened while the bat said:

In and out the bushes, up the ivy,
Into the hole
By the old oak stump, the chipmunk flashes.
Up the pole

To the feeder full of seeds he dashes,
Stuffs his cheeks,
The chickadee and titmouse scold him.
Down he streaks.

Red as the leaves the wind blows off the maple,
Red as a fox,
Striped like a skunk, the chipmunk whistles
Past the love seat, past the mailbox,

Down the path,
Home to his warm hole stuffed with sweet
Things to eat.
Neat and slight and shining, his front feet

Curled at his breast, he sits there while the sun
Stripes the red west
With its last light: the chipmunk
Dives to his rest.

When he'd finished the bat asked: "Do you like it?"

For a moment the chipmunk didn't say anything, then he said in a surprised, pleased voice: "Say it again." The bat said it again. When he'd finished, the chipmunk said: "Oh, it's *nice*. It all goes in and out, doesn't it?"

The bat was so pleased he didn't know what to say. "Am I really as red as that?" asked the chipmunk.

"Oh yes," the bat said.

"You put in the seeds and the hole and everything," exclaimed the chipmunk. "I didn't think you could. I thought you'd make me more like the owl." Then he said: "Say me the one about the owl."

The bat did. The chipmunk said: "It makes me shiver. Why do I like it if it makes me shiver?"

"I don't know. I see why the owl would like it, but I don't see why we like it."

"Who are you going to do now?" asked the chipmunk.

The bat said: "I don't know. I haven't thought about anybody but you. Maybe I could do a bird."

"Why don't you do the cardinal? He's red and black like me, and he eats seeds at the feeder like me—you'd be in practice."

The bat said doubtfully: "I've watched him, but I don't know him."

"I'll ask him," said the chipmunk. "I'll tell him what it's like, and then he's sure to want to."

"That's awfully nice of you," said the bat. "I'd love to do one about him. I like to watch him feed his babies."

The next day, while the bat was hanging from his rafter fast asleep, the chipmunk ran up the ivy to the porch and called to the bat: "He wants you to." The bat stirred a little and blinked his eyes, and the chipmunk said: "The cardinal wants you to. I had a hard time telling him what a poem was like, but after I did he wanted you to."

"All right," said the bat sleepily. "I'll start it tonight."

The chipmunk said: "What did you say I was as red as? I don't mean a fox, I remember that."

"As maple leaves. As leaves the wind blows off the maple."

"Oh yes, I remember now," the chipmunk said; he ran off contentedly.

When the bat woke up that night he thought, "Now I'll begin on the cardinal." He thought about how red the cardinal was, and how he sang, and what he ate, and how he fed his big brown babies. But somehow he couldn't get started.

All the next day he watched the cardinal. The bat hung from his rafter, a few feet from the feeder, and whenever the cardinal came to the feeder he'd stare at him and hope he'd get an idea. It was queer the way the cardinal cracked the sunflower seeds; instead of standing on them and hammering them open, like a titmouse, he'd turn them over and over in his beak— it gave him a thoughtful look—and all at once the seed would fall open, split in two. While the cardinal was cracking the seed his two babies stood underneath him on tiptoe, fluttering their wings and quivering all over, their mouths wide open. They were a beautiful soft bright brown—even their beaks were brown—and they were already as big as their father. Really they were old enough to feed themselves, and did whenever he wasn't there; but as long as he was there they begged and begged, till the father would fly down by one and stuff the seed in its mouth, while the other quivered and cheeped as if its heart were breaking. The father was such a beautiful clear bright red, with his tall crest the wind rippled like fur, that it didn't seem right for him to be so harried and useful and hard-working: it was like seeing a general in a red uniform washing hundreds and hundreds of dishes. The babies fol-lowed him everywhere, and kept sticking their open mouths up by his mouth—they shook all over, they begged so hard—and he never got a bite for himself.

But it was no use: no matter how much the bat watched, he never got an idea. Finally he went to the chipmunk and said in a perplexed voice: "I can't make up a poem about the cardinal."

The chipmunk said: "Why, just say what he's like, the way you did with the owl and me."

"I would if I could," the bat said, "but I can't. I don't know why I can't, but I can't. I watch him and he's just beautiful, he'd make a beautiful poem; but I can't think of anything."

"That's *queer*," the chipmunk said.

The bat said in a discouraged voice: "I guess I can't make portraits of the animals after all."

"What a shame!"

"Oh well," the bat said, "it was just so I'd have somebody to say them to. Now that I've got you I'm all right—when I get a good idea I'll make a poem about it and say it to you."

"I'll tell the cardinal you couldn't," the chipmunk said. "He won't be too disappointed, he never has heard a poem. I tried to tell him what they're like, but I don't think he really understood."

He went off to tell the cardinal, and the bat flew home. He felt relieved; it was wonderful not to have to worry about the cardinal any more.

All morning the mockingbird had been chasing everything out of the yard—he gave you the feeling that having anything else in the world was more than he could bear. Finally he flew up to the porch, sat on the arm of a chair, and began to chirp in a loud, impatient, demanding way, until the lady who lived inside brought him out some raisins. He flew up to a branch, waited impatiently, and as soon as she was gone dived down on the raisins and ate up every one. Then he flew over to the willow and began to sing with all his might.

The bat clung to his rafter, listening drowsily. Sometimes he would open his eyes a little, and the sunlight and the shadows and the red and yellow and orange branches waving in the wind made a kind of blurred pattern, so that he would blink, and let his eyelids steal together, and go contentedly back to sleep. When he woke up it was almost dark; the sunlight was gone, and the red and yellow and orange leaves were all gray, but the mockingbird was still singing.

The porch light was lit, and there were already dozens of insects circling round it. As the bat flew toward them he felt hungry but comfortable.

Just then the mockingbird began to imitate a jay—not the way a jay squawks or scolds but the way he really sings, in a deep soft voice; as he listened the bat remembered how the mockingbird had driven off two jays that morning. He thought: "It's queer the way he drives everything off and then imitates it. You wouldn't think that—"

And at that instant he had an idea for a poem. The insects were still flying around and around the light, the mockingbird was still imitating the jay, but the bat didn't eat and he didn't listen; he flapped slowly and thoughtfully back to his rafter and began to work on the poem.

When he finally finished it—he'd worked on it off and on for two nights—he flew off to find the chipmunk. "I've got a new one," he said happily.

"What's it about?"

"The mockingbird."

"The mockingbird!" the chipmunk repeated. "Say it to me." He was sitting up with his paws on his chest, looking intently at the bat—it was the way he always listened.

The bat said:

Look one way and the sun is going down,
Look the other and the moon is rising.
The sparrow's shadow's longer than the lawn.
The bats squeak: "Night is here," the birds cheep:
    "Day is gone."
On the willow's highest branch, monopolizing
Day and night, cheeping, squeaking, soaring,
The mockingbird is imitating life.

All day the mockingbird has owned the yard.
As light first woke the world, the sparrows trooped
Onto the seedy lawn: the mockingbird
Chased them off shrieking. Hour by hour, fighting hard
To make the world his own, he swooped
On thrushes, thrashers, jays, and chickadees—
At noon he drove away a big black cat.

Now, in the moonlight, he sits here and sings.
A thrush is singing, then a thrasher, then a jay—
Then, all at once, a cat begins meowing.
A mockingbird can sound like anything.
He imitates the world he drove away
So well that for a minute, in the moonlight,
Which one's the mockingbird? which one's the world?

When he had finished, the chipmunk didn't say anything; the bat said uneasily, "Did you like it?"

For a minute the chipmunk didn't answer him. Then he said: "It really is like him. You know, he's chased me. And can he imitate me! You wouldn't think he'd drive you away *and* imitate you. You wouldn't think he could."

The bat could see that what the chipmunk said meant that he liked the poem, but he couldn't keep from saying: "You do like it?"

The chipmunk said, "Yes, I like it. But he won't like it."

"You liked the one about you," the bat said.

"Yes," the chipmunk answered. "But he won't like the one about him."

The bat said: "But it *is* like him."

The chipmunk said: "Just like. Why don't you go say it to him? I'll go with you."

When they found the mockingbird—it was one of his good days—the bat told him that he had made up a new poem. "Could I say it to you?" he asked. He sounded timid—guilty almost.

"To be sure, to be sure!" answered the mocking-bird, and put on his listening expression.

The bat said, "It's a poem about—well, about mockingbirds."

The mockingbird repeated: "About mockingbirds!" His face had changed, so that he had to look listening all over again. Then the bat repeated to the mockingbird his poem about the mockingbird. The mockingbird listened intently, staring at the bat; the chipmunk listened intently, staring at the mockingbird.

When the bat had finished, nobody said anything. Finally the chipmunk said: "Did it take you long to make it up?"

Before the bat could answer, the mockingbird exclaimed angrily: "You sound as if there were something wrong with imitating things!"

"Oh no," the bat said.

"Well then, you sound as if there were something wrong with driving them off. It's my territory, isn't it? If you can't drive things off your own territory what can you do?"

The bat didn't know what to say; after a minute the chipmunk said uneasily, "He just meant it's odd to drive them all off and then imitate them so well too."

31

"Odd!" cried the mockingbird. "Odd! If I didn't it really would be odd. Did you ever hear of a mockingbird that didn't?"

The bat said politely: "No indeed. No, it's just what mockingbirds do do. That's really why I made up the poem about it—I admire mockingbirds so much, you know."

The chipmunk said: "He talks about them all the time."

"A mockingbird's *sensitive*," said the mockingbird; when he said *sensitive* his voice went way up and way back down. "They get on my nerves. You just don't understand how much they get on my nerves. Sometimes I think if I can't get rid of them I'll go crazy."

"If they didn't get on your nerves so, maybe you wouldn't be able to imitate them so well," the chipmunk said in a helpful, hopeful voice.

"And the way they sing!" cried the mockingbird. "One two three, one two three—the same thing, the same thing, always the same old thing! If only they'd just once sing something different!"

The bat said: "Yes, I can see how hard on you it must be. I meant for the poem to show that, but I'm afraid I must not have done it right."

"You just haven't any *idea!*" the mockingbird went on, his eyes flashing and his feathers standing up. "Nobody but a mockingbird has any *idea!*"

The bat and the chipmunk were looking at the

32

mockingbird with the same impressed, uneasy look. From then on they were very careful what they said —mostly they just listened, while the mockingbird told them what it was like to be a mockingbird. Toward the end he seemed considerably calmer and more cheerful, and even told the bat he had enjoyed hearing his poem.

The bat looked pleased, and asked the mockingbird: "Did you like the way I rhymed the first lines of the stanzas and then didn't rhyme the last two?"

The mockingbird said shortly: "I didn't notice"; the chipmunk told the mockingbird how much he always enjoyed hearing the mockingbird sing; and, a little later, the bat and the chipmunk told the mockingbird good-by.

When they had left, the two of them looked at each other and the bat said: "You were right."

"Yes," said the chipmunk. Then he said: "I'm glad I'm not a mockingbird."

"I'd like to be because of the poems," the bat said, "but as long as I'm not, I'm glad I'm not."

"He thinks that he's different from everything else," the chipmunk said, "and he is."

The bat said, just as if he hadn't heard the chipmunk: "I wish I could make up a poem about bats."

The chipmunk asked: "Why don't you?"

"If I had one about bats maybe I could say it to the bats."

"That's right."

For weeks he wished that he had the poem. He would hunt all night, and catch and eat hundreds and hundreds of gnats and moths and crickets, and all the time he would be thinking: "If only I could make up a poem about bats!" One day he dreamed that it was done and that he was saying it to them, but when he woke up all he could remember was the way it ended:

At sunrise, suddenly, the porch was bats:
A thousand bats were hanging from the rafter.

It had sounded wonderful in his dream, but now it just made him wish that the bats still slept on the porch. He felt cold and lonely. Two squirrels had climbed up in the feeder and were making the same queer noise—a kind of whistling growl—to scare each other away; somewhere on the other side of the house the mockingbird was singing. The bat shut his eyes.

For some reason, he began to think of the first things he could remember. Till a bat is two weeks old he's never alone: the little naked thing—he hasn't even any fur—clings to his mother wherever she goes. After that she leaves him at night; he and the other babies hang there sleeping, till at last their mothers come home to them. Sleepily, almost dreaming, the bat began to make up a poem about a mother and her baby.

It was easier than the other poems, somehow: all

he had to do was remember what it had been like and every once in a while put in a rhyme. But easy as it was, he kept getting tired and going to sleep, and would forget parts and have to make them over. When at last he finished he went to say it to the chipmunk.

The trees were all bare, and the wind blew the leaves past the chipmunk's hole; it was cold. When the chipmunk stuck his head out it looked fatter than the bat had ever seen it. The chipmunk said in a slow, dazed voice: "It's all full. My hole's all full." Then he exclaimed surprisedly to the bat: "How fat you are!"

"I?" the bat asked. "I'm fat?" Then he realized it was so; for weeks he had been eating and eating and eating. He said: "I've done my poem about the bats. It's about a mother and her baby."

"Say it to me."

The bat said:

A bat is born
Naked and blind and pale.
His mother makes a pocket of her tail
And catches him. He clings to her long fur
By his thumbs and toes and teeth.
And then the mother dances through the night
Doubling and looping, soaring, somersaulting—
Her baby hangs on underneath.
All night, in happiness, she hunts and flies.
Her high sharp cries
Like shining needlepoints of sound
Go out into the night and, echoing back,
Tell her what they have touched.
She hears how far it is, how big it is,
Which way it's going:
She lives by hearing.
The mother eats the moths and gnats she catches
In full flight; in full flight

The mother drinks the water of the pond
She skims across. Her baby hangs on tight.
Her baby drinks the milk she makes him
In moonlight or starlight, in mid-air.
Their single shadow, printed on the moon
Or fluttering across the stars,
Whirls on all night; at daybreak
The tired mother flaps home to her rafter.
The others all are there.
They hang themselves up by their toes,
They wrap themselves in their brown wings.
Bunched upside down, they sleep in air.
Their sharp ears, their sharp teeth, their
        quick sharp faces
Are dull and slow and mild.
All the bright day, as the mother sleeps,
She folds her wings about her sleeping child.

When the bat had finished, the chipmunk said: "It's all really so?"

"Why, of course," the bat said.

"And you do all that too? If you shut your eyes and make a noise you can hear where I am and which way I'm going?"

"Of course."

The chipmunk shook his head and said wonderingly: "You bats sleep all day and fly all night, and see with your ears, and sleep upside down, and eat while you're flying and drink while you're flying, and turn somersaults in mid-air with your baby hanging on, and—and—it's really queer."

The bat said: "Did you like the poem?"

"Oh, of course. Except I forgot it was a poem. I just kept thinking how queer it must be to be a bat."

The bat said: "No, it's not queer. It's wonderful to fly all night. And when you sleep all day with the others it feels wonderful."

The chipmunk yawned. "The end of it made me all sleepy," he said. "But I was already sleepy. I'm sleepy all the time now."

The bat thought, "Why, I am too." He said to the chipmunk: "Yes, it's winter. It's almost winter."

"You ought to say the poem to the other bats," the chipmunk said. "They'll like it just the way I liked the one about me."

"Really?"

"I'm sure of it. When it has all the things you do, you can't help liking it."

"Thank you so much for letting me say it to you," the bat said. "I *will* say it to them. I'll go say it to them now."

"Good-by," said the chipmunk. "I'll see you soon. Just as soon as I wake up I'll see you."

"Good-by," the bat said.

The chipmunk went back into his hole. It was strange to have him move so heavily, and to see his quick face so slow. The bat flew slowly off to the barn. In the west, over the gray hills, the sun was red: in a little while the bats would wake up and he could say them the poem.

High up under the roof, in the farthest corner of the barn, the bats were hanging upside down, wrapped in their brown wings. Except for one, they were fast asleep. The one the little brown bat lighted by was asleep; when he felt someone light by him he yawned, and screwed his face up, and snuggled closer to the others. "As soon as he wakes up I'll say it to him," the bat thought. "No, I'll wait till they're all awake." On the other side of him was the bat who was awake: that one gave a big yawn, snuggled closer to the others, and went back to sleep.

The bat said to himself sleepily: "I wish I'd said we sleep all winter. That would have been a good thing to have in." He yawned. He thought: "It's almost dark. As soon as it's dark they'll wake up and

I'll say them the poem. The chipmunk said they'd love it." He began to say the poem over to himself; he said in a soft contented whisper,

> A bat is born
> Naked and blind and pale.
> His mother makes a pocket of her tail
> And catches him. He clings—he clings—

He tried to think of what came next, but he couldn't remember. It was about fur, but he couldn't remember the words that went with it. He went back to the beginning. He said,

> A bat is born
> Naked and blind—

but before he could get any further he thought: "I wish I'd said we sleep all winter." His eyes were closed; he yawned, and screwed his face up, and snuggled closer to the others.